D1352537

Juliet Jones
and the Ginger Pig

Stories from Aberteg

Sue Reardon Smith

Sue Reardon Smith

Gomer

For Harry Gibson and James German,
my father and grandfather.
I'm sorry it has taken me so long.

First published in 2018
by Gomer Press, Llandysul, Ceredigion SA44 4JL
www.gomer.co.uk

ISBN: 978 1 78562 283 0

A CIP record for this title is available from the British Library.

© Copyright: Sue Reardon Smith

Sue Reardon Smith asserts her moral right
under the Copyright, Designs and Patents Act, 1988
to be identified as author of this work.

All rights reserved. No part of this book may be reproduced,
stored in a retrieval system, or transmitted in any form
or by any means, electronic, electrostatic, magnetic tape,
mechanical, photocopying, recording or otherwise
without permission in writing from the above publishers.

This book is published with the financial support
of the Welsh Books Council.

Printed and bound in Wales at
Gomer Press, Llandysul, Ceredigion

CONTENTS

JULIET JONES
AND THE GINGER PIG

Juliet Jones lived on a farm in the mountains of Aberteg with her mum and dad, grandma and four big brothers. She loved animals, and had her own rabbit called Primrose. There were two cats called Bod and Singer, and Boyo the sheepdog. There were lots of sheep, pigs and chickens too.

Sometimes Juliet felt lonely. The farm was not near any of her friends and she was too small to go about by herself. Her brothers were quite a bit older than her, and if they weren't working for exams, they had to help their dad on the farm. They loved their sister, and had been thrilled when she was born, but they simply had no spare time to give her. Morgan, known as Mog, was the next brother up from her. He spent time with her sometimes.

Juliet was laying the table one day in the big farm kitchen and her mother was busy cooking as usual. Even Mog hadn't had much time for her lately, and Juliet was a little sad.

'Mum, why are my brothers so much bigger than me?' she asked. 'When I go to tea with Jenny from my class, her brothers aren't nearly that big and we often all play together,' said Juliet. It wasn't the first time Juliet had asked her mother this.

Her mum sighed. 'Go and tell your dad his tea is on the table,' she said. So once again, Juliet didn't get an answer.

The one person who always had a lot of time for Juliet was her grandmother. She lived in a cottage next to the farmhouse. Juliet's dad had been the farmer for so long that even Juliet's oldest brother couldn't remember their granddad, who had died a long time ago. Grandma Jones was tall with lots of white curly hair. Children in the village thought she looked just like a witch in a picture book. She and Juliet went for walks and Grandma told Juliet all about plants and the medicines that her mother – Juliet's great-grandmother – had made from them, as there was no such thing as a chemist in her day. Grandma often said to Juliet, 'You are a great comfort to me, Juliet Jones.'

Over the Easter holidays, something wonderful happened. Cousin Rachel was chosen to be May Queen at the Village Fair. She asked Juliet to be her flower girl and ride with her when she went to be crowned. Juliet's grandma went off on market day and came back with lovely material the colour of bluebells to make her dress. Her father promised to lend his tractor and trailer as the May Queen's carriage and decorate it with greenery and flowers and put hay bales on top to make seats for Juliet and Rachel.

One night after Easter, a litter of pigs was born in one of the pigsties. The next morning Juliet woke up to hear her dad calling her – he knew she liked to see the newborn piglets. Juliet hurried out and looked over the wall into the sty, but this time something was different. The mother pig was pleased with her new babies, but one little one was really small – much smaller than the others. He kept being pushed out of the way by his brothers and sisters. Juliet took one look at him and knew he was special.

'Hello, little pig!' she called to him. 'You're just like me. The smallest in the family. Don't you worry. I'll look after you.'

Juliet reached down and the little pig pushed his nose against her fingers.

'Look, Dad, he understands what I am saying!'

Juliet's dad smiled at her, but went back to caring for the sow and her other piglets. Juliet knew that he wouldn't want to spend time looking after the little pig – she would have to do it all on her own. As Mog hadn't gone back to school yet, she asked him to help her feed the little piglet until he was big enough to look after himself. Mog said he would. After that, if anyone was looking for Juliet, they went to the pigsty. She spent hours talking to the little pig. She said he understood every word.

While Juliet was busy with her piglet, Grandma Jones was busy sewing. She was making Juliet's blue dress, and one for Rachel which was white with a blue cloak. She bought blue dye to dye Juliet's shoes and blue ribbon to trim their dresses and the bunches of flowers they were going to carry.

Before long the holidays were over and it was time to go back to school. Juliet was glad to be with her friends again. The pig was big enough to be left on his own; Mog wasn't going back to school for a few days and would keep an eye on him.

On the day before May Day, Juliet went down to the kitchen for breakfast before Mog walked her to school. Everyone stopped talking when she walked into the room, which was odd. Then she heard her grandma say:

'Owen, let well alone. Don't spoil things now, leave it till next week?'

'No, Mam, I can't do that. I've always been honest with my children.'

At this point he cleared his throat, looking uncomfortable. 'Juliet, I'm taking this litter of pigs to sell at the mart next week, and that means all of the pigs – not one left behind. You're a farmer's daughter and I know you'll understand.'

But Juliet didn't understand. She had thought

that she and the pig would be friends forever. How could her dad be so horrid to her? She sat down, but ate nothing and didn't look at anyone. It was an awful breakfast. Finally, Mog nudged her arm.

'Time to go, Juliet.'

Her head hanging down, she followed him out of the door.

Going down the lane, Juliet burst into tears. This upset Mog, but what could he do? It was a sad walk to school.

When they arrived, Juliet asked her brother, 'Please Mog, can you come and fetch me when school is done? You're the only one I want to talk to.'

Mog promised he would, and even said he would bring his pocket money to buy Juliet some sweets on the way home.

That day was a long day for Juliet. Her best friends, Sian and Jenny, were worried about her. She had hardly said anything all day and although they kept asking her, she wouldn't tell them what was wrong. After lunch she sat under a tree in the playground and thought and thought about what she could do to save her pig.

When Mog came to get her, she was looking better. When they reached the main street, she asked Mog if he had brought his money.

'Yes, he told her. 'What sweets do you want?'

'No, Mog,' she said. 'I don't want sweets. I've decided how to save my pig and I need your help. If my pig doesn't look pink like Dad's other pigs, no one will want to buy him and he can stay with us forever. Grandma bought some blue dye for my shoes and I want some dye to colour my pig – any colour but pink.'

Mog was not happy about this plan.

'I don't think we want to dye him with the sort of dye Grandma used – it would be bad for his skin,' Juliet said. 'But hair dyes would be fine and not hurt him. We'll go to the chemist and buy one.'

They walked up the street to the chemist. The chemist and his assistant knew the Jones family well. They were pleased to see Mog and Juliet.

'Hello, you two, what would you like today?'

Juliet stepped up to the counter. 'Please can you show us some hair dyes?' she asked.

'Who is it for?' asked the chemist.

'It's . . . for one of the family who wants a new hair colour,' Juliet told him.

The chemist brought out some dyes and showed her the colours on the packets.

'What colour is that one?' Juliet asked, pointing at a packet. 'It looks like the leaves on our beech trees. I think I like that one.'

'That's called auburn,' said the chemist.

The chemist and his assistant looked at each other. Mog knew what they were thinking. They were thinking of his mother's pretty fair hair or his grandmother's wild white hair being dyed auburn – whatever that was. But he handed over the money, and he and Juliet left the shop.

'Now what?' said Mog.

'Well,' said Juliet. 'You feed the pigs in the evening so no one will know if my pig is missing. When no one is looking, take him to the Sulking Shed, and we will dye him, and then take him back before he is missed. When Daddy goes to see them, it will be dark and he won't notice.'

The Sulking Shed was an old cattle shed in the middle of the fields. In turn all the Jones children had rushed off there when they were upset, and that's how the shed got its name. It wasn't used for much else, and would make the perfect hiding place.

That evening, after the pigs were fed, Mog got the little pig out to the Sulking Shed without being noticed. He read the instructions on the packet while Juliet got water and old towels ready so that they wouldn't get dye on their clothes. The little pig was glad to see them.

Mog mixed up the colour. 'We'll use this old glove and rub it in. You do that, Juliet, while I pour it over him. It says "don't put near eyes", so I am going to bandage his eyes with my handkerchief.'

The combination of thick dye and cold water sent the pig rushing round the shed, but Juliet had managed to cover most of him. Only his covered-up eyes and his squiggly tail were still pink. After ten minutes they poured clean water over him, took off the handkerchief and left him to dry. Juliet gasped when she saw what colour her pig was.

'His coat is the same colour as Charlie Phillips' hair!'

And he was a bright ginger colour nearly all over. He looked very odd. The pink stripe where the handkerchief had been made him look even odder.

They got back to the farm in time for Juliet to have a bath and go to bed, and Mog promised he would put the pig back with the others when it got dark.

The next day was bright and sunny. May Day at last! Juliet came down to breakfast feeling happy. She was going to be a flower girl and she had saved her pig. Then she heard a roar:

'Juliet Jones, come here this minute!'

Dad and Grandma were looking into the pigsty. The little pig looked an even brighter ginger in the sunshine.

'What on earth do you think this pig looks like?' shouted Mr Jones.

Before Juliet could answer, her grandma said: 'I think he looks a bit surprised.'

'Surprised? Not nearly as surprised as everyone will be next week at the mart when they see him. Everyone will laugh at him and at me, and what sort of money will I get for a ginger pig with a pink stripe and a pink tail?'

Juliet couldn't believe it. He was going to take her pig to market no matter what he looked like!

'Oh, please, please, don't take him with the others! I'll be really good if you let me keep him, and I'll do all the nasty jobs around the farm.'

'Give me one really good reason why I should keep him?' her father asked.

Juliet closed her eyes, struggling to think what to say. How could she make them understand how important this was to her? It was unusual for her to be lost for words, but she certainly was at that moment. She had never before felt responsible for another person or animal, and it had made her feel really good and important. It had made her feel less lonely.

'Because he's a great comfort to me,' Juliet said at last.

It was very quiet. She opened her eyes. Dad and Grandma were looking out to sea. That was funny. There was nothing to see – not even one boat. Then they turned around. They were both smiling at her. She knew it would be all right.

That was the best day Juliet had ever had. As if by magic, all her brothers came back from where they had been working on the farm to help decorate the tractor and trailer. Grandma picked bunches of bluebells and tied them up with the blue ribbons. Soon it was time to go and Juliet went to change into her new clothes. Just as she was getting onto the tractor, Mog came out with the ginger pig. The pig had one of Boyo's collars on with some blue ribbons woven through it – he was going too! Grandma plaited the stems of three bluebells and stuck them in his collar. Off they went to collect Rachel.

After Rachel had been crowned, Mr Jones drove the tractor down the main street, and then to the rugby field for tea and games. There were lots of people in fancy dress. Everyone had come out into the streets to cheer. Juliet saw Jenny and Sian and Jenny's mum waving to her. Charlie Phillips, a boy in Juliet's class with hair as red as her ginger piglet, ran behind the tractor shouting and laughing at the pig. But Juliet didn't mind – nothing could spoil her day. As they turned into the rugby field, Mog was standing on the gate and he shouted out louder than anyone.

'Three cheers for the Ginger Pig!'

Everyone shouted and cheered louder than ever, but the little pig, who would always be called Comfort, had had quite enough excitement in the last two days to last any pig several lifetimes. With the three bluebells hanging over one eye, he was fast asleep.

DABBY DAVIES GROWS UP

Dabby Davies wasn't just small. He was extremely small. Everyone made fun of him. Well, all the other children at Aberteg School did, and that felt like everyone. He wasn't sure if the grown-ups laughed at him too, but he wasn't going to take any chances. He just stuck close by his mam and dad and his sisters. There he felt safe.

Dabby loved living by the sea. He couldn't swim, but he liked to go to the beach and sit in the sand dunes. Mari, his sister, took him there.

'Mari, look at our village over there,' Dabby said to her one day by the sea. 'It looks as if a giant came here on his holidays with a big bag of buildings. Then he threw them over the river onto the mountain. I bet that's how Aberteg was made.'

'Dabby Davies, don't be so *twp*. I never heard such a soft idea,' said Mari. 'I enjoy some of your stories, but I am not sure about that one!' Dabby really enjoyed making up stories, and Mari was his favourite audience.

'One day,' Mari told him, 'you will be able to write them all down and I can say I have a famous author for a brother!'

They spent some time talking about how lucky they were to live in that village, though. Everyone said what a pretty place it was with a big beach, the river, and the ruins of an old castle on the mountain.

There was an iron bridge over the river. Dabby and his family lived in a little cottage next to it. He loved the river just as much as he loved the sea. Dabby knew all the paths along it. He knew where to find swans, otters or kingfishers. Dabby liked noticing their habits, how they moved and played. You always knew where you were with animals and birds.

People were different, though. Sometimes there were other children on the paths. That was bad as they used to laugh and shout at him:

'Dabby, poor little dab! Shall we throw you back in the water? Don't know why your mam didn't do it.'

The one who yelled at him most was Charlie Phillips. Charlie had red hair and he was big. He and Dabby had both been born on Christmas Day.

'I bet Charlie got my share of being big,' Dabby complained one day to his mother. He was in the kitchen, watching her cook. 'It's not fair.'

Dabby's mother tutted at him with sympathy, but kept chopping vegetables.

Dabby wasn't meant to be born as early as he was. Mari always said he spoilt her Christmas. His dad had rushed up the little streets to get Auntie Bethan, the nurse. When Dabby was born, Auntie Bethan came out of her sister's bedroom, shook her head, and said to his dad:

'Well, David Davies, you've got your boy, but he's a poor little dab and no mistake.'

And the name had stuck. He was actually

named Ivor, after his granddad but no one ever called him that. Dabby was Dabby from Christmas Day onwards.

For weeks he was so small he could fit into Mari's dolls' clothes, which didn't please Mari very much. Dr Evans called and said there was nothing wrong with him. Dabby wasn't ill, he was just small. And even when he grew, he stayed small.

At first, he didn't know he was not as big as the other children his age. But when his little sister Caitlin turned two, she was the same size as Dabby – and he was four. Mari was always telling him he was small.

The January after he was five, he went to school. Mari was in the top class so they could walk to school together, but soon she would be going to big school. Miss Eynon, his teacher, looked kind. She even gave him a desk near the front of the room, because he was so much smaller than everyone else.

Dabby soon settled into school. The lessons were easy, but playtime was horrible. Children pushed him and called him nasty names. Some of the bigger boys thought it funny to pick him up and throw him to one another, as if he were a ball. He hid in the cloakroom, or he stayed behind in class to help Miss Eynon clean up the classroom. Dabby was very glad when the holidays came and he could stay at home. The big children all lived in the village, but if he was clever he could avoid them.

Then in the summer things got worse. Charlie, one of the biggest boys, and a few of his friends began to wait for Dabby in the bushes. They jumped out to frighten him when he passed by. He never knew where they would be next. After a week of this, Dabby told his mam he wasn't going out any more. He crawled under the kitchen table and curled up into a ball.

Dabby's mother wasn't having any of it. 'Out of here, my boy!' she told him. 'I need to wash the floor. Take this food basket up the mountain to Uncle George. If you don't want to go into the village, Mari will come with you to show you the way.'

Dabby had never seen much of Uncle George. Walking was very hard for him, so he didn't come down to the village much. Mam and her sisters helped Uncle George quite a bit. They cleaned his cottage, did his washing and took him food. Dabby was a little scared about meeting Uncle George on his own, but anything was better than meeting Charlie.

No one came near them as they walked up the lanes. This was no surprise; no one messed with Mari. When they came to the top lane near the mountain, Mari turned to go back to the village to find her friends. Dabby was left to face Uncle George on his own. He went up to the cottage and knocked on the wooden door.

'Come in,' said a voice.

Dabby went in. It was dark inside. Dabby could just see a small man sitting by the fire.

'Hello, Uncle George. How are you?' said Dabby, feeling nervous.

'Mustn't grumble,' came the voice again. 'Which one are you?'

'I'm Dabby,' Dabby answered.

'Not much of a name. You're called Ivor, aren't you? For my father.'

Dabby nodded. 'But no one ever calls me that.'

He unpacked the food. Uncle George's eyes lit up when he saw the lemonade and biscuits set out on the table.

'Well, I think we could both do with having some of that,' said Uncle George.

'Tell me about school, Ivor,' he asked as they ate.

So Dabby did. Slowly at first, then more and more as Uncle George listened. Dabby wasn't used to having anyone but Mari listening to his stories, even the ones that weren't made up. So he told Uncle George all about his lessons and his teacher, and even about Charlie and his friends. Dabby told him everything – good and bad. Uncle George laughed.

'What's so funny?' said Dabby. 'I can't see what's so funny.'

'Look at me, Ivor.'

Dabby wanted to say that his mam said it was rude to stare, but she also said he must always be polite, and Uncle George had asked him to look. So he looked and said nothing.

'What do you see, Ivor?' asked Uncle George. 'Did you notice that I'm small too? My head won't stay up properly. One leg is so bent I have to drag it behind me. You think you have a bad time! Things are only awful if you decide they are, Ivor.'

Dabby could see what he meant. Uncle George must have had a much harder time of it than he had. Maybe he shouldn't have gone on about school so much. But not talking about Charlie didn't make Charlie go away, and talking to Uncle George had made Dabby feel better. For a while.

'Get along home with you now,' Uncle George was saying. 'It's getting late and I don't want your mam to be cross with me for keeping you.' But all the same, he told Dabby that he could come again whenever he wanted. Dabby said that he would.

And so he did. Every day of the holidays Dabby walked back to the cottage. He took clean washing or food with him. He got wood for the fire. He picked the vegetables and fruit that Uncle George had grown. Every day when he went in, he asked his uncle how he was.

'Mustn't grumble,' he always replied.

Dabby could think of lots of things Uncle George could grumble about. When he was a boy, his brothers had taken him to school sitting on a piece of wood fixed onto old pram wheels. But Uncle George didn't seem upset about any of it.

'Never let being different stop you,' he told Dabby. 'I know you do well at school. If you work hard, when you grow up you can be anything you want to be.'

'Never mind growing up,' said Dabby. 'I'd just like to grow at all! Then maybe the boys wouldn't call me names or toss me about. Maybe I could even have friends of my own.'

Uncle George looked sad for a moment, then cross, then determined. They were going to do something about that. He would have a Plan of Action ready for Dabby's next visit.

Dabby didn't think anything could help, but he came back the next day ready to listen. Uncle George said he had it all worked out, and they were now going to think about this Charlie Phillips.

'I'd rather not, if you don't mind,' said Dabby.

'Listen to me, boy,' said Uncle George, leaning forwards a bit in his chair. 'That Charlie is a bully. And bullies are cowards. He needs to be part of a crowd to make him feel important. The other boys all follow him. If we can sort out Charlie, I bet they won't give you any more trouble. When you run away from them, it makes them feel strong. Show them you're strong too. Law of the jungle.'

Dabby wasn't sure about the last bit. Neither he nor Uncle George had even been to England, let alone a jungle.

'You don't have to fight Charlie,' Uncle George went on. 'Just don't look scared when you see him. Be confident. And you might try making some friends, too,' Uncle George added.

'Friends?' said Dabby hesitantly.

'There are other boys and girls in this school of yours, aren't there?' asked Uncle George. 'Are they all as mean as Charlie?'

'Well, no . . . at least I don't think so.'

'Good. You could do with some nice friends. And if Charlie sees you're not always alone, maybe he won't think of you as small and weak anymore.'

'Well, that's worth a try, I guess,' Dabby said.

Uncle George gave him a reassuring smile. Dabby tried to smile back.

On his way home one day after going to see Uncle George, Dabby bumped into Wyn Evans who was taking his dog for a walk. They walked along together. They had become quite friendly since Dabby's aunt, the district nurse, had taken him to meet Wyn. Wyn's dad was the local doctor and Aunt Bethan worked for him several days a week. Wyn was a quiet boy too and they both seemed to like the same puzzles and games.

When they got nearer to Dabby's cottage, he said goodbye to Wyn and turned to go home. He hardly noticed the bushes in the lanes now, though Charlie and his friends still sometimes tried to jump out and scare him. Dabby was thinking about what he would tell Uncle George on his next visit when he heard voices.

'You are a stupid, lazy boy! You have had all holidays to be a better reader, and now I find you have wasted all your time playing. I've a good mind to stop you playing rugby next winter.'

'Please, Dad, don't do that! Please don't. Anything but that.'

It was Charlie! And his dad didn't sound too happy. Dabby was closer now. He could see Charlie crying and running away from his house. But Charlie didn't see Dabby and ran straight into him.

'Hello, Charlie,' said Dabby, hoping Charlie wouldn't notice that his voice didn't sound very brave.

'Push off,' said Charlie. 'You're the last person I want to see, you little teacher's pet. Get out of my way before I knock you off the path.'

Wiping his eyes with the backs of his hands, he stuffed his fists into his pockets and walked off.

Dabby followed him. He followed him for about five minutes, and then ran to catch up with him, hoping that Charlie was feeling calmer.

'Charlie?' said Dabby. 'Are you all right?'

'I can't believe you're still here. Can't you get it into your thick head that I want nothing to do with you?'

Dabby decided to stick it out. 'I can help you make sure your dad doesn't stop you playing rugby.'

Charlie stopped and turned around. This was worth thinking about.

'Reading's the problem, isn't it?' Dabby asked.

'Yes, it is,' Charlie moaned. 'It's all right for you. Only one more week to go. I should have been doing reading every day, but I hate it. I'm no good at it. Our new teacher, Mrs Jenkins, will go mad. My brother says she is strict. I was trying not to think about it, and then my dad comes home from work early, catches me and decides to test me.'

Dabby took a deep breath. It was now or never.

'I will help you with your reading every day before we go back. But if I do, then you and the others have to stop calling me names and jumping out at me. And I don't ever want to be used as a rugby ball again.'

Charlie didn't answer for a minute or two. Then he looked down at his feet and mumbled that he would give it a try.

Instead of going home, Dabby ran straight to tell Uncle George. It was hard to know which of them was the more excited.

It wasn't easy going at first – Charlie was

angry and sulky, and Dabby had to be very patient. But when Charlie saw that Dabby wasn't going to make fun of him for being so bad at reading, he started to really work. Things got much better after that. Sometimes the lessons were even good fun.

Finally the day came to go back to school. Charlie and Dabby were both happier than before. Because of Dabby's help, Charlie could read more easily, and Dabby knew that Charlie would keep his promise. There would be no more bullying. Maybe his troubles weren't over, but it was a start. As he looked over the stone wall at the edge of the schoolyard, he saw Charlie. He waved. Charlie waved back. Suddenly Dabby felt even better. It wasn't because Charlie had waved to him. It was because he knew that before the summer holidays, he couldn't see over the school wall at all. He was growing at last!

Mrs Jenkins met him at the door of his new classroom.

'Good morning,' she said. 'How are you today, Ivor?'

'Mustn't grumble,' he replied.

SIAN LLOYD'S
WINNING HIT

Mr Lloyd was the grocer and lived above his shop, which was just up from the village square. His wife had died when his daughter, Sian, was a baby, so Mr Lloyd's mother had come to look after them both. Behind the shop was a long garden where Mrs Lloyd grew a lot of fruit and vegetables.

Sian was a happy girl apart from one thing: she was terribly clumsy. Sian was always tripping over things, or dropping them. She had hoped that when she got older it would get better, but instead it got worse – and people seemed to delight in pointing it out. If someone tells you that you are stupid, or clumsy, or no good at games for long enough, it's very hard not to believe them. This is what happened to Sian.

One day she was helping her grandma pick raspberries, holding up a big basket for the fruit to go in. When it was nearly full, Sian dropped it. Her grandma had laughed, tousled Sian's hair, and told her father about it that evening.

Since then, Sian's dad would often greet her by saying, 'Hello there, raspberry dropper!' He thought it was funny. Sian did not.

One night when Sian was going to bed, she heard her dad say to her grandma, 'That child has got two left feet. If there was a leaf on the path, she would trip over it.'

Sian looked down at her feet, sticking out the bottoms of her pyjamas. She didn't see the knot in the wood floor, and tripped over it.

'See what I mean?' she heard her father say.

But Sian's two feet looked quite normal to her, just like anyone else's – one right one and one left one.

Being clumsy made Sian scared about playing games. In the summer, when they played rounders at school, she worried about dropping the ball or falling over. To make matters even worse, her dad was really good at sports. He had been a cricketer, and still loved to tell stories about those days.

'Have I ever told you about the time I hit a six on the village green at Pontypridd?' he would say, a far-off look in his eye.

His mother and daughter always said that he had, but Mr Lloyd always went ahead and told them anyway.

Sian was in Miss Eynon's class at school, and her best friend was Juliet Jones. One day in the summer term, Miss Eynon told her class they were going to have a picnic on the big beach. There would be swimming and a rounders match. Juliet knew Sian hated games and felt very sorry for her. Miss Eynon said that the picnic was coming over to the beach in Mr Lloyd's van. This was bad news for Sian, who would be much happier if he was serving in his shop and not watching her when she was playing rounders. That was the last thing she wanted to happen.

'Don't look so miserable, Sian,' said Juliet. 'Come to the farm and spend as many Saturdays as you want. I'm sure the boys will play rounders with us and help you get better.'

'Thank you, Juliet,' said Sian. 'I'll come, but I don't think it will work. I have to help a bit in the shop first, though.'

In the middle of the next Saturday morning, Mog Jones came to collect Sian for a trip to the farm. When he walked into the shop, Mr Lloyd was serving Mrs Phillips. Charlie Phillips, her son, was with her. Charlie was in Miss Eynon's class, the same as Sian. Suddenly, there was a terrible crash of tins falling from the back.

'Oh, you've got Sian helping you, have you, Mr Lloyd?' Charlie called out, laughing.

Mrs Phillips was cross with her Charlie, but Sian had heard what he said.

She left the shop quietly and walked up the mountain with Mog, to where Juliet had marked out a rounders pitch in one of the fields. Sian missed the ball every time Mog threw it to her. Mog and Juliet tried to help, but it was no use. Sian was left-handed, and the things that worked for other people never seemed to work for her. Maybe that's what her dad had meant by 'two left feet'. She wondered if things would have been different for her if she had been born right-handed.

Mog gave her the bat and bowled at her. Again, she couldn't hit a thing. Then Grandma Jones came out of her cottage.

'I've been watching you from the window,' she said, 'and I've had enough of this. All this is no good for Sian. I'm left-handed too and a good tennis player – let me see if I can help. Here, Sian – I'll hold the bat and we'll do it together.'

It seemed they spent hours and hours with Mrs Jones holding the bat with Sian. They hit balls up the mountain until Mog and the others were tired out. Everyone was glad when Juliet's mum said that there was food in the kitchen. They did even more hitting that afternoon. Sian threw balls too – on that Saturday and two Saturdays after. At the end of the last Saturday, she could finally see a difference. Sian was hitting and catching the ball well. She didn't fall over once.

'I hope she can do it in the match,' Mog whispered to Grandma Jones.

Sian was so pleased. Maybe she wouldn't ever

be clumsy again! Surely she was ready for the rounders match.

The day of the picnic was bright and sunny. Miss Eynon and her class walked down the path by the river. Dabby Davies' mum was hanging out some washing. She rushed out and gave Dabby his swimming things, which he had forgotten. Wyn Evans smiled at Dabby; he knew that Dabby had left them behind because he didn't want to go in the water. Mr Rees the boatman was waiting for them. He waited every day to ferry anyone who wanted to go over to the big beach in one of his boats. He charged one penny at low tide and two pennies at full tide. He had his big boat today because there were so many people to take, but he would still have to make two trips. Mrs Price, Mostyn's mum, was helping Miss Eynon, so she went in the first boat. When they got to the other side, they walked up the beach. They were all carrying their swimming things. Miss Eynon said that they should have a swim before tea, which would soon be arriving in Mr Lloyd's van. Then they would play rounders to warm up.

Sian enjoyed swimming. She never felt clumsy in the water. She had so much fun that she almost forgot about the rounders match. Sian looked up to the road leading down to the beach. There was no sign of her dad. She hoped that he would come after the teams had been picked. She didn't want him to see her being picked last, as she was sure she would be.

Miss Eynon told Charlie Phillips and Mostyn Price to pick two teams. Sian was the last to be picked by Mostyn. Dabby was the last to be picked by Charlie. Charlie's team went in first, and made two rounders. Sian managed to get the ball, and threw it back to the bowler. That hadn't been too bad. Then her team went into bat. They needed three rounders to win the match. She looked up the road, and there was the little white van coming down onto the beach. Oh dear, what terrible timing!

Mostyn went in first, and scored a rounder. Mansel scored another one straight afterwards. Then lots of people were caught out. Finally, Sian's turn came. She heard the van stop on the beach. Her father must be coming over to watch, but she didn't dare look. She gripped the bat hard. She breathed slowly like she did when she was swimming. Grandma Jones had said that was sure to make her calmer.

'Just imagine you're in the water, dear,' Grandma Jones had said. 'Move as easily as you do when you swim.'

Sian watched as Charlie bowled the ball to her – it seemed to be coming very fast. She gave it an enormous hit. Because she was left-handed, everyone was waiting for the ball in the wrong place. The ball went over towards the sand dunes. Sian ran and ran, hoping she wouldn't fall – and she didn't! There was a big cheer as she made a rounder too – which meant they won the match. She heard a voice behind her:

'Well done, my girl!' her father called. 'That was tidy. You are a real chip off the old block.'

There he went again, saying something that Sian didn't understand. She thought that being a chip off something sounded a bit painful. The main thing, though, was that her dad was pleased with her.

By then, Miss Eynon and Mrs Price had

unpacked the picnic. It was laid out on big tablecloths. Mr Lloyd sat down and had tea with everyone. She heard him say to Miss Eynon that he thought that girls should play cricket as well as boys. He would like to teach both the boys and the girls. They could have a boys-against-girls match next year. Sian and Juliet looked at each other. After all, rounders was one thing, but could they learn to play cricket?

'Don't worry, Sian,' said Juliet. 'We've got a whole year to practise.'

MANSEL ROBERTS BREAKS THE RULES

Mansel Roberts was the third child of the vicar of Aberteg. He thought he had the worst position in the family. He wasn't the eldest, who was a girl, nor was he even the eldest son. He wasn't the baby either. If his mother told the younger ones to go to bed early, or the older ones to go shopping for her, he got caught whichever children she chose. He wasn't unhappy, but sometimes felt he didn't get as much attention as the others.

All Mansel's parents wanted was for their children to be safe, well and happy. Reverend Roberts was very busy – not just in Aberteg, but at a church over the mountain as well. Mrs Roberts helped her husband a lot, doing things like arranging the church flowers. She loved playing the clarinet and went with her husband in the car when he visited people. She played with the windows down so that everyone could hear.

'Mansel, as your mum is married to the vicar, is she practising to be an angel?' asked Mostyn, one of Mansel's friends.

'Don't be daft,' Mansel answered. 'She'd be playing the harp or a trumpet if that were true.'

Some people thought she was trying to block out the sound of the vicar practising his sermon.

When Mansel's father had any spare time, which wasn't often, he liked to go looking for birds. He was particularly keen on owls, and Mansel was too. Not that long ago, they had gone along the marshes down by the river because the boatman who rowed the ferry over to the big beach told them he was sure that he had seen a pair of short-eared owls. Apart from seeing the birds, Mansel liked these little trips because he got his dad to himself for a while.

One very ordinary Sunday in the summer, they all went to church as usual. It was the only day of the week when Mrs Roberts seemed to mind how clean and tidy the children were. They all sat in the front pew. Their father gave the sermon. As usual, when he got excited, he pulled hard at his left ear, and looked down from the pulpit to see his four children pulling their left ears too – even the baby, who was only two. On the way out from church, Mansel heard his name and turned to see who was speaking.

'Mansel, I think we have a pair of owls in our barn,' Farmer Jones was saying to him. 'My mother and I have both seen them.' Farmer Jones' daughter Juliet was in the same class as Mansel at school. He knew how Mansel felt about birds, and invited him to come up and see the owls when he could.

Mansel thanked him very much. He couldn't wait to tell his father! Maybe they could go that afternoon.

'Sorry, boyo, I have to go over the mountain to see someone who's ill.'

His mum said she was going with him. His sister Elin said she was taking baby Geraint to her friend Mari's for the afternoon. His brother

Gwyn said he was going to play football with his friends. And Mansel knew he wasn't to go up the mountain on his own. Overlooked again! Upset and disappointed, Mansel rushed off to his room.

After about an hour, he heard them all leave the house. His aunt, who lived with them, called up the stairs.

'Are you all right, Mansel? I am going to do some gardening.'

'I'm staying in my room to read,' Mansel called back to her. He was still sulking.

Mansel watched his aunt take her basket of tools down to the garden. Now he had to decide. If he stayed at home, he might never see the owls. They might go to another barn. Should he go up the mountain anyway? Mansel was never, ever disobedient. For the first time in his life, he was thinking about doing something he had been forbidden to do. But the thought of seeing the owls was just too much for him. He let himself out of the house. There was no one to be seen as he went up the back streets to the path that led onto the mountain.

The quickest way to get to the Jones' farm was along a path that ran just below the mountain. This was the one path that Mansel knew he shouldn't use. It was covered with bracken and had lots of big holes in it. It was hidden from the farm and the village, so if anyone fell into any of the holes, it could be a long time before they were found. But Mansel told himself he was disobeying anyway, so he might as well make a good job of it. Along the forbidden path he went. The big barn was the first bit of the farm he would come to, which was a good thing as he didn't want any of the Jones family seeing him out on his own.

It was summertime and there were a few people walking up the mountain. They were probably 'Visitors', as local people called them. Mansel could see one man about halfway up the mountain leaning on a rock, smoking a cigarette. There had been no rain and the bracken was really dry. It could burn very quickly if anyone dropped a match or a cigarette. He saw the man throw the cigarette down and move off down the path the opposite way to which Mansel was walking. Mansel shouted and waved to him to tell him to stamp out the cigarette, but the man either didn't hear or didn't care and was soon out of sight. Mansel started to run up the mountain to where the man had been sitting, but before he could reach the place, he could see smoke coming up from the ground. Then some flames appeared! Mansel began to run back down the path to the farm. It only took him five minutes, but already he could see the wind making the fire bigger. It was sweeping towards the barn.

When he reached the farm yard, he couldn't see anyone. He ran across the yard and hammered on the front door.

'Hurry, Farmer Jones, hurry! There's a fire on the mountain and it's coming this way!'

There was no answer. What would he do if no one was anywhere around? He supposed he could fill some buckets from the tap in the yard, but just one boy wouldn't be able to stop a fire.

The front door finally opened and the farmer stood in the doorway looking a bit sleepy. He soon became alert when he heard what Mansel was saying. He rushed to phone for the fire engine, but that would take time. Something would have to be done before that.

'Go and fill as many buckets as you can find in the yard,' Farmer Jones directed Mansel. 'There are several in the pigsties and some more in the shed. I will call as many people as I can to help.'

It seemed like forever to Mansel, but after about ten minutes Mr Jones' family and the villagers who lived in the lanes just under the mountain all began to appear in the farmyard. It had only needed a few phone calls, and then they had told all the people they could find – couples out for walks, children and old people. By this time, Mansel had filled all the buckets he could find and lined them up by the farmyard gate. Soon everyone had made a human chain that reached from inside the yard to the mountain, refilling all the buckets and passing them on to everyone else. The fire seemed horribly close to the barn. They all worked incredibly hard to put the fire out. At last they heard the fire engine bell ringing.

'Hurray, hurray!' they cheered.

Everyone watched as the firemen finally put out the flames. When the fire was really out and he was sure it wouldn't start up again, the chief fireman asked Mr Jones how the fire had started. Mr Jones called Mansel over and told him to say what had happened.

The fire chief was full of praise. 'What a lucky thing it was that you were out on the mountain at that time, and were sensible enough to keep an eye on that man. If it wasn't for you, it is hard to say what damage would have been done.'

Mansel was just beginning to wonder if Mum and Dad would be as pleased as the fireman when he saw his father coming across the yard, looking cross. Before he could say anything, both the fireman and Mr Jones told him that Mansel had saved the mountain and the farm buildings from being burnt. Then Mansel's mum turned up. They had been coming home when they saw the fire engine. What a surprise to see their son was there too! Mr Jones and his dad filled his mum in on what had happened.

'Mansel, you dirty little *mochyn*,' she fussed.

'Your face and hands are filthy, and just look at the state of your shoes!'

Mansel knew that he must really look a mess, because his mother never noticed things like dirty shoes. He was definitely in trouble.

'I never did get to see the owls,' he said mournfully.

Farmer Jones said that, with all the noise and fuss going on, he thought it might be days before the owls allowed anyone to see them again. But he promised that the minute he did see them, he would tell Mansel and his dad so that they could come up straight away.

When they got in the car, Mrs Roberts turned round to Mansel.

'You were bad to go out when we told you not to,' she told him, 'but it was good that you saved the barn – and a lot more besides! We won't stop you going to see the owls, as long as you are with your father. But every night this week after school, you will have to do jobs in the house with me or in the garden with your aunt.'

Mansel thought it could have been a lot worse,

so he just nodded. He was just glad that he would still get to see the owls.

Although it wasn't far to the vicarage, Mrs Roberts picked up her clarinet and started playing. Then Mansel knew things were still fairly all right, because she only every played the clarinet when she was happy.

THE BEVAN TWINS
AND THE ARTIST
ON THE MOUNTAIN

'I'm not sure I like being a twin,' said Hannah Bevan, to no one in particular. 'Why wasn't Huw a girl, or me a boy? One of each is not much good. Hywel and Dafydd Jenkins in Miss Williams' class look just like each other. No one knows which is which. Everyone always muddles them up. That would be fun.'

This was often the subject of conversation at meal times in the Bevan household. Mr Bevan was the Aberteg blacksmith and always very busy. He and his wife had twin six-year-olds, Hannah and Huw, and a small boy of two called Trefor. This morning at breakfast, Hannah was at it again, complaining.

'Think what a fuss the twins who run the teashop make of you, Hannah,' said her mum.

But the twins who had the teashop were really old. Hannah couldn't imagine them ever being young. And anyway, they were both girls – or they had been once upon a time.

'I must go,' said Mr Bevan. 'I have several horses to shoe this morning, and at noon Farmer Jones is coming to discuss his new gates. Hannah, come down then as well. Maybe you can do some drawings for the gates too.'

Huw said he would like to come along too. He loved animals, and liked being there when the horses were having new shoes. Hannah was always keen to go to the forge, especially when her father was drawing plans for making gates or fire grates. Mr Bevan would have liked to be an artist, but the Bevans had always been the blacksmiths in Aberteg. He quite often asked Hannah to help draw plans. Hannah, unlike her brother, loved painting and drawing. Huw much preferred to be out playing football.

Both twins went to see their father in the middle of that morning. Huw calmed the horses, holding their heads and whispering quietly to them as their new shoes were put in place, while Hannah sat in a corner and did some drawings of gates, ready to show Farmer Jones when he arrived.

Farmer Jones came in with his daughter Juliet and, after looking at all the drawings, decided he liked Hannah's best. Mr Bevan didn't mind a bit.

'Well, Hannah,' said Farmer Jones, 'when the gates are put up, you must all come and have tea at the farm. And we will always call them Hannah's Gates.'

Hannah was thrilled to hear this and even Huw seemed a bit pleased for her, though he didn't say anything.

There was one thing about having a brother just the same age: he wasn't going to beat her at anything. Anything Huw could do, Hannah could do too. There was great competition between them. As soon as he learned to read, she learned to read. As soon as she learned to swim or to ride a bike, he did too. And so on. She hated him being better at anything. Hannah also had a temper, and Huw liked to tease her. His favourite remark if she ever did anything well was: 'Not bad – for a girl.'

Every time he said it, Hannah went mad. One day, Hannah overheard Huw trying to teach Trefor to say, 'Not bad – for a girl.' Hannah threw herself at her twin and pulled his hair hard. Huw cried out and reached for Hannah's hair. In came their mum.

'That is quite enough!' she said. 'Perhaps you can both do something for me. I would like you to go and pick some blackberries. There are plenty on the lane up to the mountain. Be sure to stay together.'

So, each carrying a basket, they walked up past the church. Then they went along the lane below the old castle and up the lane to the mountain. It was hard walking, and very steep, but they picked lots of blackberries. Finally, the twins turned to go home, but down the lane towards them came a goat. The goat wore a head collar with a rope attached. Huw gave Hannah his basket and grabbed hold of the rope.

'You know whose goat this is?' Huw asked his sister. 'It belongs to that bad-tempered old artist.'

'The one who shouts at us and waves a stick whenever we walk past his cottage?'

'That's the one,' Huw replied. 'We had better take her back to him.'

Hannah wasn't a bit keen, but they couldn't leave the goat to walk into the village. She carried the baskets and Huw pulled the goat along behind him. The artist was looking over his gate when they got near his cottage. He had a little white beard – a bit like a goat's, actually – and he wore a beret. He had a very cross look on his face. When he saw they had his goat, he looked less cross, and came out to meet them.

'Thank you for bringing Marion back,' he said to them both. 'Please, come in and we will put her back in the field. And tell me your names.'

Huw and Hannah told him their names, and he said that he was called Professor Grunwald. They walked round the cottage. He showed them the studio where he painted. It was a big room with large windows.

'My sister draws and paints,' said Huw. 'She's not bad, for a girl.'

'What do you mean, not bad for a girl?' said the professor. 'Being an artist is the important thing! A good painting is good, no matter who paints it.'

The professor was looking cross again. Huw was glad when they reached the field on the other side of the cottage. Mrs Grunwald was feeding two other goats. She was pleased that the runaway goat was home again. Marion was always biting through her rope and going off on her own. Huw asked Mrs Grunwald if he could help feed the goats. The professor said he would show Hannah the studio. The room was full of very big paintings with very bright colours. The artist said that he used oil paints to paint them. Hannah said she would love to try oils, but they cost a lot of money.

'Come and have tea with us on Saturday,' said the professor. 'My wife will make her special chocolate cake for you. Huw can help with the animals, and you can show me some of your drawings.'

So that is just what they did. They had a wonderful afternoon. Professor Grunwald said Hannah's drawings were very good.

'There's a big competition for children in London,' he told her. 'You should enter. The prize is an easel and oil paints. I will help you.'

So the twins went up there every Saturday afternoon. Huw was a great help with the goats and chickens, and Hannah started a painting for the competition. She painted the view down the mountain, looking out of the big window. When the painting was finished, the professor packed it up for her and sent it off. Then Hannah felt sad, not just because she had enjoyed doing the painting so much, but because there would be no more visits up the mountain.

'Goodbye, Mrs Grunwald,' said Hannah as they went out of the cottage door. Mrs Grunwald looked down and saw that Hannah was looking a bit tearful, so she told them, 'You must come again whenever you like.'

They went back several times, and then things got really busy for Christmas. Hannah forgot all about the competition. Their mother had them making decorations, preparing mince pies, and buying and packing presents for all the family and friends. They were also both in a school play and had lines to learn. There just weren't enough hours in the day.

There was only a week left before school broke up for the Christmas holidays when Hannah came down to breakfast at the same time as the postman put the letters through the door. She picked them up and put them on the kitchen table in front of her dad. Letters that came to the house were always for him.

'Well, Hannah, there seems to be a letter for you today too,' he said.

A letter for her? This was unheard of except on her birthday, which wasn't for ages.

'Go on, my girl,' her dad urged, 'hurry up and open it. We all want to know what is in it.'

So she opened it and said with a huge smile on her face, 'I don't believe it! I just can't believe it! I won the competition!'

They were all so excited for her. Even little Trefor banged his spoon hard on the tray of his high chair. In the middle of all the noise, Huw patted his sister on the back:

'Not bad,' he said.

'Don't you mean, for a girl?' asked Hannah.

He gave her a big grin and replied:

'No. Not bad at all!'

WYN'S WINTER SWIM

Wyn Evans was the doctor's son and he had been ill all summer. After Easter, he had come home from school feeling dreadful. His dad said he had rheumatic fever and that he must stay home from school and rest. But that was weeks ago, and Wyn was very fed up. He enjoyed school and he didn't enjoy feeling ill.

One morning before starting his morning surgery, Wyn's father came to bring Wyn his morning medicine. He found Wyn staring sadly at the ceiling.

'Doctors' children shouldn't get ill,' Wyn said. 'Your patients will think you're not a good doctor if your son is ill for a long time.'

'Nonsense, Wyn, it's not like that at all,' said Dr Evans, handing the medicine to Wyn. 'Doctors' children get ill as much or as little as anyone else's. I am really sorry, but you will just have to be patient.'

Wyn had to stay in bed for almost a month. He read every book that he had. People gave him jigsaws and more books. He read those too, and put together all the puzzles. The weather got very warm, and Wyn kept his bedroom windows open. It made him sad to hear his friends calling for him to come outside.

'Wyn has got dramatic fever,' his sister Eleri was telling them. 'He can't come out to play for ages and ages.'

Finally, his mother said that he was well enough to sit in the window of his bedroom so that at least he would have things to look at. Dr Evans' patients came to see him in a big room at the back of the house called the surgery. Every day they came up the path, and waved to Wyn before they went to see his dad. One person he saw all the time was Sister Rees. She was the nurse and came in most days. Then she went off again on her bicycle with the big basket on the front, carrying everything she needed.

Someone else who came often was Marged,

who lived in a cottage on Farmer Jones' farm. She was a sad person who had no friends, just four scruffy dogs that went with her everywhere.

'Poor Marged,' said Wyn to his dad one morning as he took his medicine. 'Can't you make her better?'

His dad sighed. 'Really Wyn, she is lonely more than ill, and won't talk to anyone except me and Sister Rees. Her parents died when she was very young. She was married once to a young man from the village, but they had only been married a year when he went to sea. His ship was wrecked, and he and all the other sailors drowned.'

'Poor Marged,' Wyn said again.

Wyn was well in time to go back to school in September. Luckily, he had read so many books and done all the work sent by the school, so he didn't have to stay down in class. He could move on with the rest of his friends.

Staying in bed for so long had made him grow a lot, and now he was really tall. His best friend was Dabby Davies, who lived at the bottom of his road. Nurse Rees was Dabby's aunt and had brought him up to be with Wyn when Wyn was getting better. Dabby had grown a bit in the holidays too, but he was still much shorter than Wyn. They both knew that they looked funny going down the street together.

In the Christmas holidays, they went off for walks. Wyn had one sister and Dabby had two, so they both liked getting out for a bit of peace. One cold day they decided to go past Dabby's house, along the sea wall and up to the cliffs. Nobody else was about. As they were passing Dabby's house, Sister Rees rode out onto the lane ahead of them. The two boys shouted into the wind at her.

'Hello, Sister Rees!'

'Hello, Auntie Bethan!'

Sister Rees was a big woman with a big bottom. From behind, her bicycle looked very small. The boys looked at each other and laughed, holding their hands over their mouths so Sister Rees wouldn't hear.

But her voice carried back to them on the wind: 'Behave yourselves, boys! And Wyn Evans, put that scarf right round your neck! We don't need you getting ill again.'

The boys were amazed. How did she know that they were laughing? How did she know that Wyn hadn't put his scarf round his neck? She hadn't turned around at all! Dabby's mum always said she needed eyes in the back of her head to keep an eye on her children. Sister Rees was her sister. Perhaps Dabby's mum knew something about her that no one else did.

The boys carried on with their walk, but now the wind was getting very strong. They walked across the path along the sea wall and watched the big churning waves. It was nearly high tide and there was absolutely no one else to be seen. They stopped to look at the water where lots of boats were kept in the summer.

'You know, Dabby,' said Wyn, 'the thing I missed most this summer was going out in Dad's boat. I had only had last summer sailing with him. He had to know that I could swim properly before he would let me into the boat.'

'I can't really swim at all,' replied Dabby. 'I am afraid people will laugh at me because

I look so thin and small, so I always try not to go in the water.'

They went up the path past the coastguard's cottage. As they came to the top of the hill, they heard an awful noise. They ran the rest of the way to a little pebbled beach. There they saw Marged, holding three dogs on ropes, crying and shouting. She grabbed Wyn and pointed to the bay. On a rock cut off by the water was the smallest of Marged's dogs. He was shivering and howling. She said Taff had got out of his collar and rushed after a seagull. He was too frightened to try to swim back to her.

Wyn dragged Dabby down the little steps in the side of the wall leading onto the beach. There was not much beach left, just a small strip of pebbles.

'Quick, Marged, throw me the lifebelt tied on the post next to you!' Wyn cried.

On the side of the path was something that looked like a solid white tyre with a strong rope attached to it. Marged threw it to Wyn, who tied the end of the rope to an iron ring in the wall. Thank goodness his dad had taught him how to tie knots. He gave Dabby his jacket and the rope, and put the lifebelt over his head.

'You're mad, Wyn!' said Dabby. 'You've only just been ill! Let me go.'

'Don't be daft, Dabby. You'd disappear under the first wave. You said yourself that you're not a good swimmer. I promise you I am well now. Maybe it's a good thing I have grown so tall. I can walk some of the way out.'

Taking off his shoes, he marched into the water. The waves were rough and bitterly cold, and soon the water so deep that Wyn had to start swimming. He knew Dabby was right – the cold water might make him ill again. He did not at all like the thought of spending more weeks tucked up in bed, but what could he do? Dabby couldn't swim. The dog couldn't get back by itself. And the thought of Marged losing her dog felt even worse than the thought of more time off school.

Wyn could feel the tide starting to turn. It was hard work swimming out to the rock. Taff had stopped howling and was watching Wyn coming towards him. Wyn put one hand on the rock and, when the waves stopped for a second, he grabbed the dog. He held him as high up as he could.

'Quick, Dabby, pull us as hard as you can!' shouted Wyn. 'I can't really swim holding Taff, so you'll have to get us to the beach.'

Poor Dabby pulled as hard as he could, but things were against him. The tide had turned and the water was pulling out to sea, and he really was small and not very strong. His feet kept slipping on the pebbles, and he was trying hard not to cry.

Then he heard a marvellous sound: Auntie Bethan's bicycle bell. Her voice followed, calling down to him.

'What are you two boys up to now? I knew you'd want the help of a big, strong person like me one of these days. It's happened sooner than I thought.'

Dabby realised she must have known they were laughing at her being fat. She really must have eyes in the back of her head, and she seemed to know when they were in trouble too. He would say sorry to her as soon as he could, as he knew what it was like to be laughed at. He gave her the rope to pull, and ran off to the coastguard's cottage to get someone to telephone for Dr Evans.

When he came back, Wyn was out of the water, shivering and wrapped in his aunt's coat. Marged was putting Taff back on a lead and saying thank you all the time. Sister Rees told her to get back up the mountain, and light a good fire in her cottage to dry her little dog.

'Come on boys, let's go and meet Dr Evans and then he can take you home,' Sister Rees said to Wyn and Dabby. 'Dabby, you tell my sister not to be cross at the state of you. I'll call down later to tell her the whole story.'

Dr Evans was parking his car in the lane next to the coastguard's cottage, when Sister Rees and the boys came around the corner. He jumped out of the car and rushed to his son with a big blanket.

Wrapping it round him, he said: 'I know you missed out on swimming this year, Wyn, but would you mind waiting till next summer before you go into the water again?'

Wyn was still so cold he couldn't speak, so he just nodded very hard instead. Wyn felt sure he wouldn't get ill again. He would be back at school with his friends again soon, and now he had the promise of next summer to look forward to.

MOSTYN PRICE
FINDS HIS FATHER

Mostyn Price was an only child. His father had been a soldier and had died in the Second World War. He never came home again after Mostyn was born. Mostyn and his mum lived in a cottage near where Wyn Evans, the doctor's son, lived. The two boys often walked to school together. His mother worked for Mr Williams, the headmaster. She told Mostyn she kept the pencils sharpened, the inkwells full of ink and typed all the letters.

Mrs Price had a big picture of her husband in uniform on the Welsh dresser in the hall, so Mostyn knew what he looked like. But apart from that, he didn't know much. He had tried to ask his mum questions, but she didn't seem to want to talk about her husband. Being without a father was quite hard on Mostyn.

Mostyn's best friend was Mansel Roberts, the vicar's son. Mostyn spent a lot of time at the Roberts' house, and one day he asked Reverend Roberts:

'Mr Roberts, why won't my mum talk about my dad?'

'Sometimes it takes a long time, Mostyn,' Mr Roberts answered him. 'You will just have to wait till your mother is ready. One day she will be.'

So Mostyn waited, but it was not easy.

There were times that felt worse than others. One of these was a Fathers and Sons football or cricket match in the village. Mr Lloyd the grocer was kind and always asked Mostyn if he could play with him. He said he would be pleased to, as he only had a daughter, Sian, and so couldn't play otherwise. When all the other boys were shouting, 'Come on, Dad,' Mostyn felt silly shouting, 'Come on, Mr Lloyd,' and so he didn't shout anything at all. Mr Lloyd had been a friend of Mostyn's dad when they were boys, and said he had always wanted to be a soldier. Mostyn wondered if his dad would have changed his mind if he had known he was going to be killed.

Mostyn's grandparents lived in the village too. His grandma always cooked all his favourite cakes when she knew he was coming. She showed him lots of photos of his father and his aunt when they were little.

'Gran, what was my dad like?'

A lovely boy, just like you.'

That wasn't much help either. He thought if he knew all the things his father liked doing, he would feel a bit closer to him, especially if they liked to do the same things.

Mansel's dad was kind to Mostyn. If they were going off in the car somewhere, they asked him to go with them. Dr Evans took him sailing, and Farmer Jones always asked him to help with the haymaking – so things could have been worse. Mostyn just wished very much that he had actually known his own dad, and that they had been able to do things together.

'Come on Mostyn! Up you get, sleepyhead. Time to get ready for school.'

Mostyn's mum said this to him almost every morning. He found it very difficult to get up when he was told. He always said to himself that five minutes more in bed wouldn't make any difference, and that he wouldn't be late. But sometimes those five minutes were often just the five minutes that made him late. On those days, Mrs Price let him cycle to school so that he could get there faster. She said it didn't look good if the secretary's son was always late for school. Because she had to be at school early, Mostyn's mother always called up to him if he hadn't appeared before she left, and told him his breakfast was on the table. Then she hoped for the best.

One morning he was in bed half asleep when he heard his mum call. 'Mostyn, get down here at once! Don't worry to dress. Hurry up!'

What on earth was happening? It was too early for him to get up. The postman had just put some letters through the letterbox. The postman called at the same time every day.

When he heard the letterbox go bang, Mostyn knew he had half an hour more in bed. Mostyn went downstairs to find his mum looking very flustered. She was holding a letter in her hand. She read it out to him. He couldn't believe what he was hearing. Mrs Price left at once to show the letter to Mr Williams.

Mostyn got ready and had some breakfast, but he didn't feel like eating much. He was even early for school, which was very unusual indeed. Mrs Jenkins thought he seemed too quiet. Usually he was one of the most talkative boys in the class.

Every morning the whole school marched into the Big Hall. Mr Williams said prayers, his wife played the piano and everybody sang. Then they all marched out back to their classrooms. This morning when they had finished singing Mr Williams looked down from the platform and spoke to everyone.

'Sit down, children; I have something very important to tell you. Now, you all know Mrs Price and Mostyn. Mr Price died fighting for his country. Today Mrs Price has had a letter from London. Mr Price (he was also called Mostyn) has been awarded the Victoria Cross for being very brave. One day he was in a safe place away from the fighting, when he saw three wounded soldiers. They were not in a safe place, so he went back three times to save them. Sadly, he was killed himself on the last trip back to safety.'

Mostyn could feel his friends looking at him. His face got redder and redder. He looked at his mother on the other side of the room with all the teachers. She was looking a bit pink herself.

Mr Williams carried on. 'Mrs Price will be going to London to get the medal from the King. She will be taking Mostyn with her. Today we are all very proud. Because of men like Mr Price – or should I say, Corporal Price – we live in a better and safer world. Tomorrow the school will have a day's holiday. I am going to make sure that somewhere in this village there will be a plaque so that the name of Mostyn Price will always be remembered.'

By this time Mostyn didn't know what to do. Back in the classroom all his friends rushed up to him and thumped him on the back, telling him how great his dad was.

Things weren't the same after that. Everyone wanted to tell him things about his dad. He knew which games his dad liked playing. He knew what food he liked, and where his favourite places were. Some days he thought he ought to take a notebook out with him to collect all the stories. And the funny thing was that his mum seemed to want to talk too. At last he was getting to know his dad, even though he wasn't here anymore. In some ways, it seemed, he was like his dad, and in other ways he wasn't like him at all, but now that really didn't matter.

Mr Williams kept his promise. People gave a lot of money so that Mr Price would be remembered. So much money came that there was enough for a statue. Mrs Price said she knew her husband would have to be in uniform, but she would rather he wasn't holding a gun. The statue was put at the top of the rugby field, with a big square stone underneath it. The words on the stone meant that everybody could read about Mr Price. The figure was looking down to the river, and out to sea. He was holding one hand up to his eyes, like he was blocking out the sun.

With the other hand, he was leaning on a forked stick. Mrs Price said it couldn't have been in a better place. Her husband had loved rugby, and the view out to sea was the one he liked best.

Mostyn had a wonderful time in London. They stayed with his uncle, who was a policeman. He took them to see lots of places, like the Tower of London. When they came home, Mrs Price put the medal on the dresser next to her husband's photograph. She loved showing it to anyone who came to call.

People stopped talking about his dad after a little while, but Mostyn didn't mind. He was so much happier. One thing hadn't changed, though. He still couldn't get up in the morning. He asked everyone if his father had always been late too, but they said he had always been early. So his mum said being late was his own fault and no one else's, and now Mostyn didn't mind at all.

Some mornings, he was up in time to walk to school with Dabby Davies and Wyn Evans. Other mornings he got out his bike and cycled up the road. Luckily the school was only a few streets away. The rugby field was further up from Mostyn's house, on the other side of the road. Mostyn had to pass his dad's statue every morning, and he liked that. He would look across the field to see the bronze figure holding a walking stick. As the other hand was up in the air, Mostyn liked to think that his dad was waving to him. So he would wave at the statue and, quickly looking round to see that no one could hear him, he would shout: 'Morning, Dad!'

AUTHOR'S NOTES

Aberteg is based on Newport, or Trefdraeth as it is also known, on the coast of Pembrokeshire, a place that has been very important to me all my life. I was the same age as my Aberteg children when I first went to stay there a few years after the Second World War ended, and I have spent time there every year since then. Several of the adult characters are based loosely on people I knew. The German artist in 'The Bevan Twins and the Artist on the Mountain' was inspired by the previous owner of our cottage, and Uncle George by our nearest neighbour a couple of fields away.